BENNY'S BAD DAY

Written by Michael J. Pellowski
Illustrated by Doug Cushman

Troll Associates

Library of Congress Cataloging in Publication Data

Pellowski, Michael.
   Benny's bad day.

   Summary: Starting with his alarm clock going off too
early, Benny Bear has a terrible, awful, bad day.
   [1. Bears—Fiction]   I. Cushman, Doug, ill.
II. Title.
PZ7.P3656Be   1986   [E]   85-14016
ISBN 0-8167-0620-4 (lib. bdg.)
ISBN 0-8167-0621-2 (pbk.)

BENNY'S
BAD DAY

RING!
RING! RING!
RING! RING! RING!
Benny Bear's alarm clock went
off too early.

Slowly, Benny opened his eyes.
He did not like to get up early.
He liked to sleep late.
"Be quiet alarm clock," he said.
"It is too early."

The alarm clock would not be
quiet. RING! RING! RING!
Oh what an awful noise!

Benny Bear did not want to get
up. He wanted to be in bed. But
the noise was too awful. Benny
reached for the alarm clock.

Whoops! CRASH! Out of bed he
fell. That's how Benny's bad day
began.

"It's too early to get up," Benny said. "But now my eyes are open. I cannot sleep. I will have breakfast."

"Breakfast sounds good," he
said. "Eggs and toast sound
good. I will have eggs and toast
for breakfast."
Benny went into the kitchen. He
got the eggs. Benny liked eggs.

Whoops! Benny slipped.
Whoops! The eggs slipped
too—down they went. CRASH!

There were broken eggs on the
kitchen floor. There were
broken eggs near the kitchen
door. There were broken eggs
on Benny's foot. Too bad for
Benny!
"Up early. Broken eggs. What a
day!" cried Benny. "What a
terrible, awful, bad day."

Benny put bread in the toaster.
"I will have toast for breakfast,"
he said.
Benny went to wash up.

Splash! BRRR! The wash water
was cold. Splash! BRRR! The
wash water was cold as ice. The
icy water made Benny cold.

"I'm freezing cold," said Benny.
"Warm toast with honey will
warm me up."
Benny Bear went back to the
kitchen.

Benny smelled smoke. The
smoke came from the kitchen.
The toast was too warm. It was
burned.

Off went the toaster. Out came
the toast. Oh what awful
smoke! Oh what terrible toast!
Oh what awful, smoky toast!

"No toast and honey today," said Benny. "No eggs. No breakfast. What a terrible, awful day."

Next Benny went out. He went
out to see his beehive. Beehives
are where bees live. Bees make
honey. Bears like honey. Benny
Bear liked honey a lot.

Benny liked his bees. The bees
liked Benny. Benny and the bees
were friends. But sometimes
even friends get mad. On
Benny's bad day, the bees got
mad.

Benny went up to the hive.
"Hi, bees," said Benny. "How is
my honey?"
He picked up the hive. The bees
were not feeling friendly today.
The bees were mad. They did
not want the hive picked up.

"BUZZ," said the bees.
"BUZZ! BUZZ!"
"That is not a friendly buzz,"
Benny said. "That is a mad
buzz. Oh what an awful noise
that buzz is!"

Whoops! CRASH! Down went
the hive.
"BUZZ! BUZZ!" said the bees.
Away ran Benny. The mad bees
went after him.

Benny ran to the lake. Into the lake he jumped. SPLASH!

BRRR! The water was cold. It was icy cold. Too bad for Benny.

24

Bees do not like water. Bees do not like lakes. After awhile the bees went away. They went back to the hive.

Benny came out of the lake.
Now Benny was mad. He was
icy cold.
"What a day. What an awful,
bad day," said Benny. "What
terrible thing is next?"

Benny went home. He went home to eat lunch. It was lunch time. For lunch Benny made jelly bread. Benny liked jelly bread.

Benny also took an apple. An
apple is good with jelly bread.
"This will be a good lunch,"
Benny said.

Benny went to eat his lunch
outside. He sat under the apple
tree.
"Now I'll eat my good lunch,"
said Benny.
He took out the jelly bread.

It was a good lunch. But it was a
bad day for Benny. Whoops!
The jelly bread slipped.
SPLOSH! It fell in the dirt.
It fell jelly side down.

"Jelly bread with dirt is no good," said Benny. "I cannot eat dirty jelly bread. I will eat my apple."

30

Benny started to eat his apple.
Benny looked at the bite where
he had eaten. Something was
there. Something was in Benny's
apple. What was that something?

"A worm!" cried Benny. "A worm is in my apple. Wormy apples are not good to eat. That makes me mad."

Benny's jelly bread was in the dirt. His apple had a worm in it. His lunch was no good. Too bad for Benny.

"Up too early," said Benny.
"Broken eggs! Icy wash water!
Burned toast! No breakfast! Mad
bees! A cold lake! Dirty jelly
bread! A wormy apple! No
lunch! What a terrible, awful,
bad day!"

Suddenly, Benny felt tired. He had gotten up too early. He needed a nap.

"I will sleep in the warm sun," said Benny.

Benny went to sleep.

Benny slept and slept. He slept
in the warm sun. But the sun
was too warm. It burned
Benny's nose.

Benny Bear woke up. His nose
was sunburned. It was burned
badly!

Benny went home. He washed
his burned nose with cold water.

Benny Bear was mad. He was so
mad he didn't eat. He went to
bed. Going to bed early is good
on an awful, bad day.

The next day came. It was not
an awful, bad day. It was a
good day. Benny Bear got to
sleep late.

The wash water was warm.

The eggs did not crash. The
toast did not burn.

Benny had a good breakfast.

Outside, Benny's bees were
friendly.

Benny picked up the hive. The
bees buzzed a friendly buzz.

Lunch was good. No dirt on Benny's jelly bread. No worm in his apple.

The sun was warm—but not too
warm. Benny did not get
sunburned.

After a very good supper, Benny
went to bed. It was cozy and
warm. Benny felt fine.

"Some days are awful, bad days," said Benny. "And some days are good, good days. Today has been a good, good day." Then he smiled and closed his eyes. He dreamed good dreams all night long.